To Ila
from: Nana

S0-BZX-629

5 Minute Storytime

Little Red Riding Hood

Charles Perrault

Retold by Jennifer Shand
Illustrated by Andrea Doss

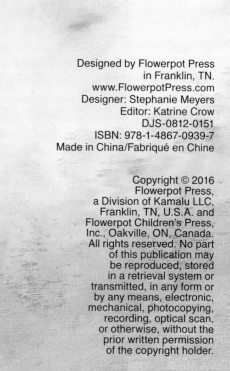

Designed by Flowerpot Press
in Franklin, TN.
www.FlowerpotPress.com
Designer: Stephanie Meyers
Editor: Katrine Crow
DJS-0812-0151
ISBN: 978-1-4867-0939-7
Made in China/Fabriqué en Chine

Copyright © 2016
Flowerpot Press,
a Division of Kamalu LLC,
Franklin, TN, U.S.A. and
Flowerpot Children's Press,
Inc., Oakville, ON, Canada.
All rights reserved. No part
of this publication may
be reproduced, stored
in a retrieval system or
transmitted, in any form or
by any means, electronic,
mechanical, photocopying,
recording, optical scan,
or otherwise, without the
prior written permission
of the copyright holder.

Once upon a time...

There was a young girl who lived in a village near the woods with her mother and father. Every so often they would travel to visit her grandmother on the other side of the woods. The young girl's grandmother always doted on her and gave her presents when she visited. The best present her grandmother gave her was a little red riding cape with a little red hood. She wore it everywhere she went and soon enough, everyone was calling her Little Red Riding Hood.

One day, Little Red Riding Hood's mother called to her and said, "Your grandmother is not feeling well. Why don't you go for a visit and take her some treats to brighten her day?"

"I would love to!" replied Little Red Riding Hood. So Little Red Riding Hood set out on the path to her grandmother's house.

As Little Red Riding Hood entered the woods, a wolf approached her. Since she did not know that he would really like to eat her up, she was not afraid of him. So they started to talk...

"Hello there, little girl," said the wolf.

"Hello," said Little Red Riding Hood.

"Where are you going all by yourself?" asked the wolf.

"Oh, I am headed to my grandmother's house. I am going to take her some treats."

"That is so very kind of you," said the wolf. "Pray tell me, where does your grandmother live?"

"She lives in the first cottage along the path, just beyond the river," Little Red Riding Hood told the wolf.

"You know what your grandmother would love?" the wolf asked, as he was concocting a plan.

"You should pick her some wildflowers to make a bouquet."

"That is a splendid idea!" replied Little Red Riding Hood.

And so she began wandering through the woods looking for the prettiest flowers she could find. That was exactly what the wolf wanted. Now he could get a head start and arrive at Grandmother's house first.

When the wolf arrived at Grandmother's house,
he knocked on the door.

"Who's there?" Grandmother asked.

"It's your granddaughter," the wolf
replied in a high-pitched voice,
trying to sound like Little Red Riding Hood.
"I have some treats for you."

"Oh, how nice!" said Grandmother.
"Pull the latch, my dear, and come on in."

The wolf burst into the room and tried to grab Grandmother, but she was surprisingly quick on her feet and managed to get away. She immediately ran off to get help.

"Oh well," thought the wolf. "I can still wait for the little girl." He looked around for one of Grandmother's nightgowns as he concocted another plan.

A short while later, Little Red Riding Hood came to the door...

When he heard the knock, the wolf once again
disguised his voice, this time to sound like
Grandmother. "Who is it?"

"It's me, Little Red Riding Hood," she replied.

"Pull the latch and come in, dear child,"
the wolf said.

Little Red Riding Hood noticed that it did not
sound like her grandmother, but she thought
perhaps her cold had changed her voice,
so she went inside. She approached her
grandmother's bed and noticed she did not
look like herself either.

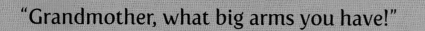

"Grandmother, what big arms you have!"

"All the better to hug you with!" the wolf replied.

"Grandmother, what big ears you have!"

"All the better to hear you with!"

"Grandmother, what big eyes you have!"

"All the better to see you with!"

"Grandmother, what big teeth you have!"

"All the better to EAT YOU UP WITH!"

And with that, the wolf jumped
out of bed and chased after
Little Red Riding Hood.

Fortunately, just then, Grandmother returned with some help from a woodcutter who was working nearby in the forest. The three of them chased the wolf out of the house, into the woods, and all the way to the river.

The wolf was running so fast that he fell right into the river, and the water carried him far, far away—and they never saw him again!

Little Red Riding Hood and her grandmother thanked the woodcutter and offered to share their treats. As they ate cake to celebrate, Little Red Riding Hood promised them that she would never talk to a wolf ever again!

The end.